For
Don & Debbie
December 25, 1996
Merry Christmas!
Love,
Edwin, Daye, McKenzie, Missy

Hallelujah!

What Men Live By
by Leo Tolstoy

As retold by Solomon M. Skolnick

Design and Illustration by Mullen & Katz

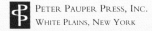
PETER PAUPER PRESS, INC.
WHITE PLAINS, NEW YORK

The text of *What Men Live By*
is based on the 1964 Peter Pauper Press edition,
and has been retold for the modern reader.

Copyright © 1996
Peter Pauper Press, Inc.
202 Mamaroneck Avenue
White Plains, NY 10601
All rights reserved
ISBN 0-88088-860-1
Printed in Singapore
7 6 5 4 3 2 1

What Men Live By
by Leo Tolstoy

Shoemaker, with his wife and children, lived in a farmer's house. He had neither house nor land of his own, and he supported himself and his family by his cobbling. Bread was dear, and work cheap; and what he made by work went to buy food. The shoemaker and his wife had one sheepskin coat between then, and that was falling into rags, and this was the second year the shoemaker had been wanting to buy skins for a new coat.

By the autumn the shoemaker had gathered together a little money; and there was money due him from the farmers in the village.

One cold morning the shoemaker got himself ready to go to the village for his sheepskin. He put on, over his shirt, the wadded jacket which his wife had made for herself, and over that his belted cloth coat; put his money in his pocket, cut himself a stick, and departed after breakfast. He thought to himself: "I shall get my money from the farmers, I'll add it to what we have saved, and I'll buy sheepskins for a coat."

So the shoemaker went into the village and stopped by at one of the farmers'; he was not at home. His wife promised to send her husband to him with the money in a week. He went on to another. This farmer swore that he had no money. He gave him only small change for mending his boots. The shoemaker thought of getting the sheepskins on credit, but the fur-dealer would not hear of it. "Bring the money," said he, "and then take what you like. We know how debts mount up." So the shoemaker made no purchases that day. He got only a trifle for mending the boots, and he took away another pair of old boots for resoling.

The shoemaker was depressed. He drank away the whole of his pocket money in vodka, and set off home without his sheepskins. He had been cold coming into town, but he was warm now from the vodka. He went on his way with one hand striking at the frozen snow-clods with his long stick, and with the other hand swinging the boots by the laces. And as he went along, he talked to himself:

"I'm warm without a sheepskin coat," said he. "I've drunk a thimbleful and it skips about through all my veins. So a sheepskin is not necessary after all. Here I go along and forget all my troubles. That's the sort of man I am. What do I care? I

can get along without sheepskins. There's one thing, though—that wife of mine will fret about it. She'll say: 'It's a shame, you work for the farmer and he leads you by the nose.' Wait a bit! If you don't bring me my money, you farmer, I'll take the very cap from your head, by God I will! What sort of pay is this? He palms off a couple of coins on me! What's a man to do with a couple of coins? Drink it up, and be done with it. 'I'm hard up,' says he. You're hard up, are you, and don't you suppose that I am hard up too? You have a house and cattle and all I have is on my back! You make your own flour, I have to buy mine. Get it from wherever I can, I have to buy flour every week. I go home and all the bread is gone. Again I have to buy flour. Why can't you give me my money, and no nonsense!"

The shoemaker went on till he came to the shrine at the corner. He looked, and close up by the shrine something was glistening white. It was just then beginning to be twilight. The shoemaker looked at it more narrowly, but he could not make out what it was.

"There's no such stone as that there!" thought he. "A cow, perhaps? But it's not like a cow either. It has got a head like a man. But what would a man be doing here?"

He drew nearer. What marvel was this? It was indeed a

man sitting there quite naked. Who shall say whether he was alive or dead? He was leaning against the shrine, and didn't move. The shoemaker felt odd. He said to himself: "They have killed some man, rifled his pockets, and left him out here. You go on, and don't mix yourself up with it!"

So the shoemaker went on. He went in back of the shrine so the man was no longer to be seen. He passed by the shrine and looked round; there was the man leaning forward, and moving a little as if he were looking towards the shoemaker. The shoemaker became still more afraid, and he thought to himself: "Shall I go up to him or shall I pass by? Go to him, indeed! Some evil may come of it! Who knows who and what he is? No good errand has brought him here, I can tell you that! Maybe he'll attack me. And even if he doesn't whatever can I do with a naked man? I can't give him the very last rags off my own back. God help me while I pass by him, that's all!"

And the shoemaker quickened his pace. He was already passing the shrine when his conscience began to speak to him. And the shoemaker stood still in the middle of the road.

"What ails the man?" said he to himself. "What are you doing, Simon? Here's a man dying in misery and you take fright and pass him by? Come, come, Simon, this won't do!"

imon went up to the man, looked carefully at him and saw that he was young and strong, but it was plain that the man was half frozen and full of fear—there he sat, leaning against the wall, and did not even look at Simon, as if he were too weak to raise his eyes. Simon went close up to him, and, suddenly, as if the man had only just awoke, he turned his head, opened his eyes, and looked at Simon. Simon threw the boots he was carrying to the ground, took off his belt, placed it on the boots, and drew off his coat.

"Can you talk a bit?" said he. "Never mind! Come, put this on!"

Simon took the man by the elbow and helped to lift him up. The man got up, and Simon saw that his body was slender and clean, that he had no bruises, and his face was pleasant. Simon threw his coat over the man's shoulders, but the man could not manage the sleeves. So Simon buttoned up the coat for him, and belted it with the belt.

Simon also took his tattered cap from his head to put it on the bare head of the man, but his own head went quite cold, and he thought to himself: "I am bald all over my head, but he has long hair," and he put on his hat again. "It would be better if I gave him the boots to wear," said he.

So he made him sit down, and put the old boots on to the man's feet.

Thus the shoemaker dressed him, and said: "There you are, brother! Come now, try and move about a bit and warm yourself. You will feel all right in a minute. Can you walk by yourself?"

The man stood up, looked kindly at Simon, but could not speak a word.

"Why don't you speak? We can't pass all of the winter here. We must be getting home. Look here now! Here's my wooden stick! Lean on it if you feel weak. Off we go!"

So the man set off. He walked easily, and never lagged behind.

As they went along the road, Simon said, "Where are you from?"

"I am not of this place."

"So I see, for I know everyone who lives here. But how

then did you come to be at the shrine?"

"I may not tell you."

"I suppose the people here mistreated you?"

"Nobody has mistreated me, but God has punished me."

"Yes, indeed—God is over all, and everywhere His hand is upon us. But where would you like to go? "It's all the same to me."

Simon was amazed. The man was gentle of speech, and not like a rogue, and yet he would give no account of himself. And he said to the man: "Look now, come to my house and warm yourself up a bit."

So Simon went on, and the stranger walked alongside of him. The drink Simon had taken was now pretty well out of him, and he began to feel freezing cold. On he went, snuffling loudly and wrapping his wife's jacket more closely around him, and he thought to himself: "You went out for a sheepskin, and you come back without a coat, and bring a naked man home with you besides. Your wife will not bless you for it!"

And the moment he fell to thinking of his wife Matrena, he grew uncomfortable. But when he looked at the stranger he remembered how the man had looked at him at the shrine, and his heart leaped up within him.

imon's wife was ready early. She chopped the firewood, brought in the water, fed the children, took a bit herself, and began to think: "When shall I make the bread, now or tomorrow?" A big piece still remained.

"If Simon has had something to eat down in town," she thought, "and doesn't eat much for supper, there will be enough bread for tomorrow."

Matrena put away the bread, and sat down at the table to sew a patch on to her husband's shirt. All the time she thought of her husband, and how he had gone to buy sheepskins for a coat.

"I hope the sheepskin-seller won't cheat him, for my old man really is very simple. He cheats nobody himself, but a little child might lead him by the nose. I went through last winter as best I could without a sheepskin coat. I could go nowhere, not even to the brook. And look now! he has left the house, and has put on every stitch we have. I have nothing to put on at all. He's a long time coming. I hope my little one has not gone astray somewhere."

While Matrena was still thinking over these thoughts, there was a scraping on the outer staircase; somebody was coming in. Matrena stuck her needle into her work, and went out into the passage. She looked. Two were there,—Simon, and with him some sort of a man without a cap, and in felt boots.

Matrena noticed the breath of her husband. "Yes, that's it," she thought, "he's been drinking." And when she perceived that he was without his long coat, in the jacket only, and carried nothing in his hand, and was silent, but pulled a wry face, Matrena's heart was hot within her. "He has drunk away our money," she thought; "he has been wandering about with some vagabond or other, and has gone so far as to bring him home with him."

Matrena let them go into the room, and came in herself also. The man was a stranger—young, haggard; the coat he had on was theirs. He stood still, neither moving nor raising his eyes. And Matrena thought: "He is not a good man, for he is afraid."

Matrena wrinkled her brows, went up to the oven, and waited to see what they would do next.

Simon took off his hat and sat down on the bench as if all were well.

"Well, Matrena!" said he, "give us some supper, come!"

Matrena grumbled to herself, but kept standing by the oven as if she never meant to move from it. First she looked at the one, and then she looked at the other, but she only shook her head.

Simon saw that his wife was very angry; but what was to be done? He pretended to notice nothing and took the stranger by the arm.

"Sit down, brother!" said he, "and we'll have some supper."

The stranger sat down on the bench.

"Come now, have you cooked anything?"

Matrena grew angry.

"Yes, but not for you. I see you have drunk your sense away. You went for a sheepskin coat and have come back without your own, and have brought back some naked beggar with you into the bargain. I have no supper to give a pair of drunkards."

"Don't judge so quickly, Matrena! Your tongue wags and wags. But first you should ask what manner of man it is."

"It is you who should say what you have done with our money."

Simon fumbled in his jacket, drew out the paper money, and unfolded it.

"The money—there it is; but the farmer has given me nothing, he said he would give it to me soon."

Matrena grew still angrier. He had not bought the sheepskins, and he had given his only coat to some naked rascal, and even brought him home with him.

She took the paper money from the table, put it in her apron, and said:

"You'll get no supper from me. You can't afford to feed all the naked drunkards you meet."

"Ah! Matrena, listen first of all to what people say to you."

"What! listen to reason from a drunken fool? How right I was when I refused to be your wife at first. My mother gave me lots of linen—you drank it away. You went to buy sheepskins—you drank that money away too."

Simon wanted to explain to his wife that he had not spent all the money on drink. He wanted to say how he had fallen in with the man; but Matrena didn't give him the chance of speaking a word or finding an answer—she spoke two words to his one.

Matrena talked and talked, and then she made a rush at Simon and caught him by the sleeve.

"Give me back my jacket! That is all I have left, and you've taken it from me and put it on your own back. Give it to me, you mangy dog!"

Simon drew off the jacket and pulled one of the sleeves the wrong side out. Then his wife tugged at it, and almost tore it at the seams. Matrena snatched up the jacket, threw it over her head, and made for the door. She would have gone out, but stopped short, for her heart was sore within her. She was seething and she wanted to know who this strange man was.

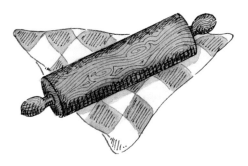

atrena stood still, and said, "If he were a good man he would not be naked like that. And if you had been about any honest business, you would have said where you picked up such a fine fellow!"

"I'll tell you then. I was going along. I passed by the shrine, and there sat this man, naked and frozen. Would he not have perished if God had not brought me to him? What was to be done now? Was it such a small matter to leave him? I took him, clothed him, and brought him home. Don't be so angry then."

Matrena would have liked to scold some more, but she looked at the stranger and was silent. His arms were clasped together on his knees, his head had sunk down upon his breast; he did not open his eyes, and his face was all in folds and wrinkles, as if something was suffocating him. Then Simon spoke:

"Matrena! is there nothing of God within you?"

Matrena heard this sentence, looked again at the stranger, and suddenly her heart was moved. She went to the oven and

got some supper. She put a cup on the table, poured out some hot soup, brought out their last piece of bread. Then she put down a knife and two spoons.

"Will you taste our bread?" said she.

Simon nudged the stranger.

"Sit here, my friend!" he said.

Simon cut the bread, crumbled it into the soup, and began to eat. But Matrena sat at the corner of the table, rested her head on her elbows, and looked at the stranger.

And Matrena felt sorry for the stranger, and began to like him. And suddenly the stranger grew more cheerful. He ceased to wrinkle his face, he raised his eyes towards Matrena, and smiled.

They finished supper; Matrena cleared away, and began to question the stranger:

"Where do you come from?"

"I am not of this place."

"Has any man robbed you?"

"God has punished me."

"And you were lying naked like that?"

"I was lying naked like that, and freezing. Simon saw and had compassion for me; he gave me his coat and asked me to

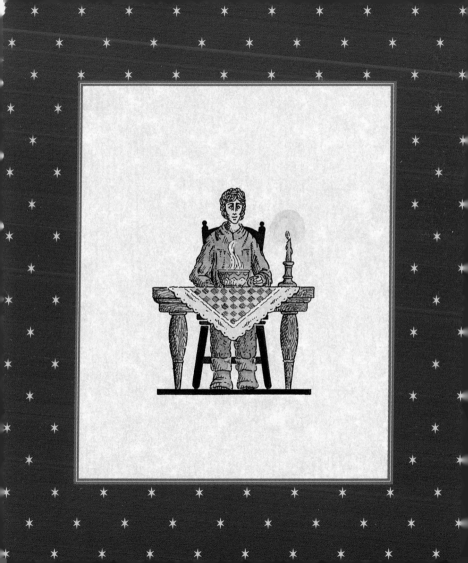

come home with him. And you have had pity upon me, and fed me. The Lord bless you."

Matrena rose up, took from the window Simon's old shirt, the same shirt she had mended, and gave it to the stranger. She also hunted up some old trousers of Simon's, and gave them to the man.

The stranger took off the coat, put on the shirt and trousers, and lay down in the loft. Matrena put out the lamp, took the coat and joined her husband near the oven.

Matrena lay down but could not sleep; she could not get the stranger out of her thoughts.

For a long time Matrena could not sleep, but lay listening. Simon also could not sleep, and drew the coat towards his side of the cot.

"Simon!"

"Eh?"

"We have eaten our last bit of bread. I have made no more. I don't know how it will be tomorrow. I'll have to borrow a little from our neighbor."

"We shall live and be satisfied."

The woman lay back and was silent.

"The stranger is a good man, that's clear, only why is he so secretive about himself?"

"Perhaps he has to be."

"We give him what we have, but why does nobody give to us?"

Simon did not know what to answer. "Just let us stop talking!" he said. Then he turned over and went to sleep.

n the morning Simon awoke. The children were asleep, his wife had gone to the neighbors to borrow flour. The stranger, in the old trousers and the shirt, was sitting on the bench and looking upwards. His face was even brighter than the evening before, and Simon said:

"What trade do you know?"

"I know nothing."

Simon was amazed, and he said,

"Where there's a will to do it, a man can learn anything."

"All men work, and I will work too."

"What is your name?"

"Michael."

"Well, Michael, you won't tell us anything about yourself, and that's your business, but you must eat. If you will work as I tell you, then I'll feed you."

"The Lord preserve you. I will learn. Show me what to do."

Whatever work Simon showed him, he understood it immediately, and after three days he worked as if he had been

at it all his life. He worked without blundering, and ate but little. He worked without a break, kept silence and always looked
upwards.

They had seen him smile only once, and that was on the
first evening when Matrena had given him some supper.

ay by day, week by week, the year went round. Michael lived at Simon's and worked. The fame of Simon's workman spread. They said that nobody could sew boots together so cleanly and so strongly as Simon's workman Michael. They began to come to Simon for boots from the whole countryside, and Simon began to prosper in his trade.

One day, in the winter-time, Simon and Michael were sitting working together, when a three-horse sleigh, with all its bells ringing, dashed up to the house. They looked out of the window; the sleigh stopped at their door; a young servant leaped down from the seat, and opened the door of the sleigh. Out stepped a gentleman wrapped up in a fur coat. He got out of the sleigh and went up to Simon's house. Matrena threw the door wide open.

The gentleman stooped his head down to pass under the doorway, and entered. When he stood upright his head very nearly touched the ceiling, and his body took up a whole corner of the room.

his boot off his left leg; then he held out his foot and said: "Take my measure!"

Simon sewed together a piece of paper, had a good look at the gentleman's foot, went down on his knees, wiped his hands neatly on his apron so as not to soil the elegant sock, and began to measure. The gentleman sat down, twiddled his toes about in his stockings, looked round at the people in the hut and perceived Michael.

"Who's that you've got there?"

"That is my apprentice. It is he who will stitch the boots."

"Look now!" said the gentleman to Michael, "be careful how you stitch! The boots must last through the whole year." Simon also looked at Michael. He saw that Michael was not looking at the gentleman, but was staring at the corner behind the gentleman as if he saw someone there. Michael kept on looking and looking, and all at once he smiled, and his face grew quite bright.

"What are you showing your teeth for, you fool? You had much better see that the things are ready in time!" said the gentlemen.

And Michael said: "They'll be ready when they're wanted."

"Very well."

The gentleman put on his boot and his fur coat, sniffed a bit and went towards the door. But he forgot to stoop, so he hit his head against the lintel. The gentleman cursed, rubbed his forehead, went down the steps, out the door, and drove off.

Then Simon said: "He is hard as rock. He nearly knocked the beam out with his head and it hardly hurt him a bit."

But Matrena said: "How can he help getting hard and tough with the life he leads? Even death itself has no hold over a rock like that."

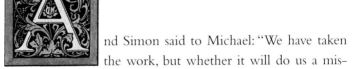nd Simon said to Michael: "We have taken the work, but whether it will do us a mischief after all who can say? The leather is dear, and the gentleman is stern. What if we blunder over it? Look now! Your eyes are sharper than mine, and your hands are defter at measuring. Cut out the leather now, and I'll work on the lining."

Michael obeyed at once. He took the gentleman's leather, spread it out on the table, folded it in two, took his knife, and began to cut out.

Matrena came forward and watched Michael cutting out, and she was amazed at the way in which Michael did it. Matrena was used to the sight of shoemaker's work, and she looked and saw that Michael did not cut out as shoemakers usually do for boots, but in a circle. Matrena would have liked to speak, but she thought: "Maybe I don't understand how gentlemen's boots ought to be cut out. No doubt Michael knows better than I. I won't interfere."

Michael had now cut out the leather, and he took up the

ends and began to sew; not as shoemakers do with boots, so as to have two ends, but with only one end, like those who make soft slippers for the dead.

Matrena was amazed at this also, but even now she didn't interfere. Michael went on sewing. Simon got up for supper, and looked around. Out of the gentleman's leather Michael had made, not boots, but slippers.

Simon groaned: "How is it," thought he, "that Michael, who has been working with us for a whole year without making a mistake, has now done us this mischief. The gentleman requires heavy soled boots, and he has stitched slippers without soles. What shall I say to the gentleman? I can never replace leather like this."

And he said to Michael: "What is this you have done, my friend? You have ruined me. The gentleman ordered boots, and what have you stitched together here?"

Scarcely had Simon begun to take Michael to task about the boots when someone knocked. They opened the door, and in came the servant who had been with the gentleman.

"Good health to you!"

"Good health! What's wrong?"

"My mistress has sent me about the boots."

"About the boots?"

"Yes, about the boots. Master needs no more boots. He's dead! He didn't even get home alive. He died in the sleigh. When the sleigh got to the house and we went to help him out, there he was frozen stiff, lying there dead. It was as much as we could do to tear him from the sleigh. My mistress has sent me, saying: 'Tell the shoemaker that since boots are no longer needed for master, would he make a pair of soft slippers for the body out of the leather.' I am to wait till they are stitched, and then I am to take them back with me."

Michael took the clippings of the leather from the table and rolled them up into a ball. He took the two slippers, which were ready, slapped them one against the other, wiped them with his apron, and gave them to the lad. The lad took away the slippers. "Good-bye, gentlemen! Good day to you."

he years passed by. It was now the sixth year of Michael's living with Simon. He behaved the same way as before. He went nowhere, and spoke to no stranger; and the whole of that time he had smiled only twice: once when Matrena first had prepared supper for him, and once when the great gentleman had come to the house.

Simon was delighted with Michael. He no longer asked where he came from; his only fear was that Michael would someday leave him.

One day they were all sitting at home. Matrena was putting an iron pot on the stove, and the children were running along the benches and looking out of the windows. Simon was stitching at one window, and Michael was hammering the heel of a boot at the other. One of the little boys came along the bench up to Michael, leaned against his shoulder, and looked out of the window.

"Look, Uncle Michael! A lady is coming with her children to our house, and one of the little girls is lame."

As soon as the boy said this, Michael threw down his work, turned to the window and looked out into the road.

Simon was amazed. Michael had not once looked into the road before, but now he had rushed to the window and was looking at something. Simon also looked out of the window, and he saw a lady coming straight towards his door; her clothing was elegant, and she led two little girls in furs, with kerchiefs round their heads. The children were as like as two peas. It was impossible to tell one from the other, only one of them was lame in one foot, and limped.

The lady went up the stairs to the passage, and opened the door. She pushed her two little children on before her, and entered the house.

"Good health, gentlemen!"

"Please come in. What can we do for you?"

The lady sat down on a chair; the children shyly pressed close to her knees. The good people looked on and wondered.

"Will you sew me leather shoes for the children?"

"I guess we can do that. We don't as a rule make shoes for children, but we can do so, of course. My Michael here is a master at his trade."

Simon glanced towards Michael, and saw he had thrown

down his work, and was gazing at the children. He couldn't take his eyes from them.

Simon was amazed at Michael. It is true they were nice children—black-eyed, plump-cheeked, rosy-faced—and their little furs and frocks were also very nice; but still Simon could not understand why Michael should look at them as if he recognized them from before.

Simon was amazed, but he began to talk to the lady, and settle about the work to be done. They arranged it, and he got ready to take measurements. Then the lady took the lame little girl on her lap, and said:

"Take the measurements from this little one. Make one shoe for her left foot, and three from the measurements of the right foot—they are twins."

Simon took the tiny measurements and said to the lame little girl:

"How did this happen to you? Were you born with it?"

"No," said the lady, "her mother did it."

Matrena then drew near. She wanted to know who the woman was, and all about the twins. "Then you are not their mother?" she asked.

"I am not their mother, nor indeed any relation, but I

adopted them. I have fed them both. I had a child of my own, but God took him; yet I couldn't love my own child more than I love these."

"Whose children then are they?"

he woman began to speak, and this is what she said:

"It is now six years ago," said she, "since the parents of these orphans both died in one week. The father died on the Tuesday, and they buried the mother on the Saturday. These poor little things were born three days after their father died, and their mother did not live out the day of their birth. My husband and I lived at that time in the village. We were their neighbors. The father of these children worked as a woodcutter. One day he was cutting a tree, and it fell right upon him. Scarcely had they brought him home than he gave up his soul to God; and his wife gave birth the same week to these two girls. The poor mother was quite alone in the house; she had neither a nurse nor a midwife. Alone she bore them, and alone she died.

"I went in the morning to look after my neighbor. By the time I came to the hut, the poor thing was already cold. In her agony she had rolled upon this little girl and broken her leg.

Other neighbors came. They washed and tidied the body; they made a grave and buried her. The children were orphaned. What was to be done with them? I was the only woman in the village who was nursing. I took the twin babies to my own house for the meantime. The farmers came together; they thought and thought what to do with the children, and they said to me: 'Maria, keep the children for a time at your house, and give us time to think the matter over.'

"At first I fed only the well child, and the one that had been injured I did not feed at all. I didn't expect her to live. But soon I thought to myself, 'How can you bear to see this angelic face pining away?' So I began to feed her also. I nourished my own and these two as well. I was young and strong, and God gave me an abundance of milk. But in the second year I buried my own child. And God gave me no more children. We live now at the mill with the grain-dealer; my husband gets good pay and our life is pleasant. But we have no children of our own. How could I bear to live alone, if it were not for these children? And how dear they are to me! Without them I would be a candle without wax."

With one hand the lady pressed the lame little girl to her side, and with the other she wiped the tears from her cheeks.

"It is plain," said Matrena, "that the proverb is true which says, 'We can live without father and mother, but we cannot live without God.'"

So they went on talking, and the woman rose to go. As the shoemaker conducted her out, the room became bright with light. They looked at Michael. He was sitting with his hands folded on his knees, he looked upwards with a smile, and there was a light all about him.

imon went up to him. "What is it, Michael?" said he.

Michael stood up and put down his work. Then he took off his apron, bowed to his host and hostess, and said: "Farewell, my host and hostess. God has forgiven me; you must forgive me too."

And the shoemaker and his wife saw that the radiance came from Michael. So Simon stood up and bowed low to Michael, and said to him:

"I see, Michael, that you are no mere man, and I am not able to keep you, nor am I able to ask you any questions. Tell me, nevertheless, this one thing—why, when I found you and brought you to my home, were you so sad; and why, when my Matrena gave you food that first night, did you smile, and from then on brighten up? Then again, when the great gentleman ordered the boots, you smiled a second time; and from that time forth you became brighter still. Now, when the lady brought these children, you smiled a third time, and grew

exceedingly bright. Tell me now, Michael, whence is this light, and why did you smile these three times?"

And Michael said: "Light comes forth from me, because although I was punished, God has now forgiven me. I smiled three times because God sent me to learn three divine lessons. I learned the first divine lesson when your wife had compassion on me, and then I smiled the first time. I learned the second divine lesson when the great man ordered his boots, and so I smiled the second time; and just now, when I saw the children, I learned the third divine lesson, and I smiled for the third time."

Simon said: "Tell me now, Michael, why did God punish you, and what are those divine lessons—so that I too may learn them?"

And Michael answered: "God punished me because I was not obedient. I was an angel in Heaven, and God sent me to take away the soul of a woman. I flew down to earth, and saw there a woman who lay sick. She had just given birth to twin girls; they moved weakly beside their mother, and she was too weak to be able to put them to her breasts. The woman saw me, and understood that God had sent me for her soul. She burst into tears, and said: 'Angel of God! They have only just buried my husband; he was struck dead by a tree. I have no one at all to bring up my poor children. Do not take away my poor, wretched soul, let me but feed and nourish my little girls till they can stand up on their feet. How can the children live to grow up with neither father nor mother?' And I listened to the mother. I laid one child on her breast, I put the other child in her arms, and I ascended to the Lord in Heaven. I flew up to the Lord, and said to Him: 'I cannot take the soul away from that poor mother. The father was killed by a tree, the mother has borne twins, and she prayed me not to take the soul out of her, and said: "Let me but feed and nourish my little children till they can stand up on their feet. How can the children live to grow up with neither father nor mother?" And so I did not take away the soul of the poor mother.' Then God said, 'Go

and fetch hither the soul of the mother, and learn three lessons. Thou shalt learn *What is given to men, What is not given to men, and What men live by.* When thou hast learnt these things, thou shalt return to Heaven.' And I flew back again upon the earth, and took away the soul of the woman. The little ones fell from her breast. The dead body fell back upon the bed, pressed upon one of the little children, and broke her leg. I rose above the village; I was carrying the soul to God. Then a blast of cold wind caught me, my wings drooped down and fell off, and the soul went alone to God; but I fell to the earth."

nd Simon and Matrena understood who it was they had clothed and fed, and who had lived with them, and so they wept for fear and joy. Then the Angel said:

"I was alone in the open field and naked. Never had I known before the needs of man; never before had I known hunger and cold, and what it is to be a man. I grew more and more hungry; I was freezing, and I knew not what to do. I looked about me; I saw in the field a shrine made for God; I went to this shrine of God; I wanted to shelter myself in it. But the shrine was locked; there was no getting into it. I sat down by the shrine to be sheltered from the wind. Evening drew on. My hunger grew; I was freezing, and racked with pain. All at once I heard a man coming along. He was carrying boots, and talking to himself. It was the first time I had seen a human face while feeling what it was like to be a man. I had a horror of this face, and turned away from it. And I heard how this man was talking to himself, and how he asked himself how he was

to protect his body against the cold of winter and provide for his wife and children. And I thought to myself, 'Here am I perishing from cold and hunger; but this man can never help me because he can only think of how he is to clothe himself against the winter and provide his family with bread.' The man saw me and was troubled. Then a still greater fear seized him, and he hurried by. I was in despair. Suddenly I heard the man coming back. I looked and could not recognize the man I had seen before. Then there had been death in his face, but now he had suddenly become a living soul, and in his face I recognized God. He came to me, clothed me, took me with him, and led me to his house. I entered his house. His wife came out to meet us and began to speak. The woman was even more dreadful than her husband had been. The spirit of death came from her mouth, and I could not breathe in the deathly air around her. She wished to drive me out into the cold, and I knew that if she drove me out, she would die. Then all at once her husband reminded her of God, and a great change suddenly came over the woman. And when she gave me some supper she looked at me, and I looked at her, and Death was no longer upon her—she was a living soul, and I recognized God in her.

"And I remembered the first lesson of God: 'Thou shalt learn *What is given to men.*' Then I knew that love has been given to men, to dwell in their hearts. And I rejoiced that God had begun to reveal to me what He had promised, and I smiled for the first time; but I was not yet able to understand everything. I did not understand what is *not* given to men, nor what men live by.

"I began to live with you, and a year went by. And the man came and ordered boots—boots that would last a year and neither loosen nor split. And I looked at him, and suddenly I saw behind him my companion, the Angel of Death. No one but me saw this Angel, but I knew him; and I knew also that before the sun went down he would take away the soul of the rich man. I thought to myself, 'This man makes plans for a year, and he knows not that he will die before tonight'; and I remembered the second lesson of God: 'Thou shalt learn *What is not given to men.*' What mankind was given I knew already. Now I knew what is *not* given to mankind. It is not given to men to know their own needs. And I smiled the second time. And I rejoiced that I had seen my companion Angel, and that God had revealed to me the second lesson.

"But I was not yet able to understand everything. I was not able to understand yet what men live by; and I lived on and waited until God should reveal the last lesson to me. Then in the sixth year came the woman with the twin children, and I knew the children, and I knew that they had been kept alive. I knew it, and I thought, 'The mother begged me to spare her to save her children, and I believed the mother; I thought that without father or mother it was impossible for children to live; and lo! a strange woman has nourished them and brought them up.' And when the woman wept with joy over another's children, I saw in her the living God, and knew what men live by; and I knew that God had revealed the last lesson to me, and had forgiven me, and I smiled for the third time."

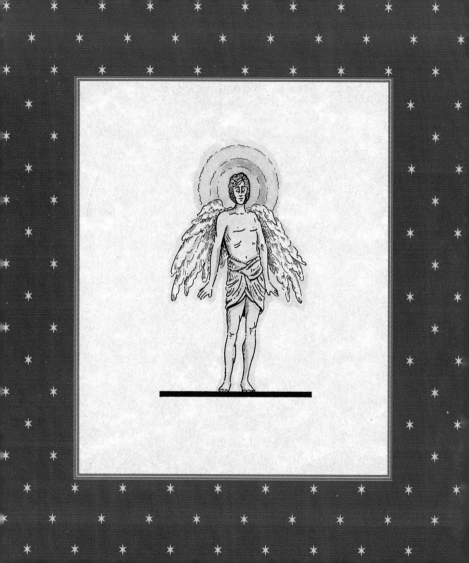

nd the clothes fell off the body of the Angel, and he was clothed with light, and he began to speak more terribly, as if his voice did not come from him, but from Heaven. And the Angel said:

"I learnt that man does not live by care for himself, but by love for others. It was not given the mother to know what was needful for the life of her children; it was not given to the rich man to know what was needful for himself; and it is not given to any man to know whether by the evening he will want boots for his living body or slippers for his corpse. When I came to earth as a man, I lived not by care for myself, but by the love that was in the heart of a passerby, and his wife, and because they were kind and merciful to me. The orphans lived not by any care they had for themselves; they lived through the love that was in the heart of a stranger, a woman who was kind and merciful to them. And all men live, not by reason of any care they have for themselves, but by the love for them that is in other people.

"I knew before that God gives life to men, and desires them to live; but now I know far more. I know that God does not desire men to live apart from each other, and therefore has not revealed to them what is needful for each of them to live by himself. He wishes them to live together united, and therefore has revealed to them that they are needful to each other's happiness.

"I know now that people only *seem* to live when they care only for themselves, and that it is by love for others that they really live. He who has Love has God in him, and is in God—because God *is* Love."

And the Angel sang the glory of God, that the house trembled at his voice, and the roof opened, and a pillar of fire shot up from earth to Heaven. Simon and his wife fell down with their faces to the ground; and wings burst forth from the Angel's shoulders, and he rose into Heaven.

And when Simon raised his eyes again, the house stood there as before, and in the house there was no one but his own dear family.